"I think you and I have more in common than we know."

Sammy's Attic by Ben Gallup

Copyright © 2021 Benjamin Gallup

ISBN: 978-1-7339661-2-2

Sammy's Attic

By Ben Gallup

Promotional Edition

1.

Walking to the first day of school Sammy's smile shined, and his happy feet bounced with each step. *Boing, boing, boing!* Walking home later, his face drooped, and he dragged his sad feet down the sidewalk. *Flop. Flop. Flop.*

This wasn't just the first day of a new school year. It was Sammy's first day at a new school.

Last night he tossed and turned in bed, every nerve buzzing with worry. He imagined everything that could go wrong. He could already see

the sour look on his teacher's face, and
he could feel the hard, silent stares of
all the strange kids.

But something about the sunrise,
a new day, clean clothes, and a bowl of
his favorite cereal had swept all the
worries from his mind. His eyes were
lit with a new spirit. Oh! The hope he
felt walking down that sidewalk in his
new neighborhood! Even the birds
seemed to sing, "There goes Sammy!
Everyone is going to want to be his
friend! What a lucky kid!"

2.

Sammy's teacher didn't have a
sour face. But she wasn't very warm or
welcoming either. It seemed like she
was as nervous as Sammy had been last
night when he was tossing and turning!
Ms. Crimini looked anxiously around
the room, wearing a sweaty sheen on
her brow, greeting the families with
awkward spurts of words. She smiled
with her mouth, but not her eyes. Her
eyes were anxious. She had the look of
a sheep about to sing for an audience of
wolves.

The kids weren't wolves though. They didn't even glare and frown at Sammy. But they didn't smile and talk to him either. The kids were too busy showing off their new shoes or wrestling against the lockers or frozen in their own lonely silence.

Sammy's new school turned out to be...school. The class played a get-to-know-each-other game, in which some students bragged, and some said as little as possible, but no one showed who they truly were. Ms. Crimini asked a freckled and spectacled student with big teeth, Roger, to pass out the old, stinky textbooks. As soon as Sammy got a whiff of the books, he felt like he was back in his old school, and a little homesick sadness washed over his face and heart

At lunch Sammy sat alone, just to be safe. At recess, Sammy shuffled around at the edge of the playground trying to act like he didn't feel awkward. In the afternoon, Sammy was tired, but he managed to keep his eyes on Ms. Crimini and pretend he was listening.

At long last the day was over. Sammy stood outside the school door for a moment, thinking maybe a friendly kid would come chat and invite him to hang out. But all the kids left, and soon the school yard grew quiet and empty.

Ms. Crimini walked out for a moment, looking exhausted and relieved, but still a little nervous.

"Oh hi, Stanny! We hope you like our school! We'll see you tomorrow," she said, smiling only with her mouth. She looked up and scanned the school yard, tensely shifting her eyes left and right, and then walked back into the building.

Sammy stood alone. The rustling sound of early autumn leaves broke the quiet in his mind and grew in his ears. He scanned the schoolyard with his own eyes, in his own calm, thoughtful way, and began walking. His feet had cheerfully carried him to school, but Sammy had to lug his feet home.

3.

"How's it going, dude? How was school?" Dad asked, making his afternoon coffee.

"It was fine," Sammy said, trying to add a cheerful edge to his drone.

"What's your teacher like? Did you make any new friends?"

"I *said* it was *fine, DAD*. Why do you have to ask so many questions?" Sammy snapped, suddenly angry.

"Jee whiz, Sammy! Where did that come from?" Dad asked. "I know it's been hard lately, but we're all in this together. I just wanted to know some details about your day, because I care about you."

Sammy felt bad and looked down. It was true. He had no reason to be angry at Dad. He thought for a moment, and realized he was embarrassed to admit that he hadn't made any friends, and that the teacher didn't even know his name. He wanted to have a great day and make Dad proud.

"Your right, Dad," Sammy sighed. "I'm sorry. Really, my teacher is fine. It's just that she seemed a little too busy to talk to me much. And the other kids were mostly like the kids back home...I mean, like the kids back in Greenhill, except they're all strangers.

I'm sure I'll make some friends before too long." Sammy felt a real bit of hope as he finished talking. He could always imagine something better, something he could even believe in. "I think I'm just going to lay in bed for a bit."

"Sounds good, my son," Dad boomed in a funny, deep voice. Sometimes Dad was a comedian.

4.

Sammy dragged himself into bed. His imagination started stirring right away. His eyes stared at the ceiling, but all he could see were the pictures in his mind.

"What if I don't make any friends? What if I'm lonely for the rest of my life? I can't believe the forest fires took everything. I wonder where the other kids go to school now. What if the fires come and take our new house too? I can't believe the forest fires took everything. I can't believe the forest fires just came. I can't believe can't believe I can't I can't I..." It was too much for Sammy to think about. He tried to shut his mind's door on the visions of blackened trees in orange blazes, and the heavy smoke that poured into the sky, which was pitch black in the middle of the day.

"Huh! What's that?" Sammy thought, noticing a square door on the ceiling of his new bedroom. It had a little handle and appeared to be a door to the attic.

Sammy rolled out of bed and walked towards the door. He carefully stood on his dresser, got on his tippy toes, reached up and

FOOM!

The door fell open with a burst of snow and a *thud* on the floor. A furry, little animal on the floor stood up and shook off the snow, terrified and looking to escape.

"Hey! What did you do to Ralph?"

Sammy looked up and saw a boy kneeling, peering down from the edge of the hole in the ceiling. The face looked a little angry but mostly worried about Ralph.

"Oh, I...I...I'm so sorry...I didn't..." Sammy stammered, baffled.

Ralph was already smiling and panting again. Sammy had never seen such a creature. It looked like a mix between a dog, a cat, and something else Sammy couldn't figure out.

"Who...who are you, and why are you in my house, and why is there snow up there?" Sammy asked.

"I'm Tu. Is there a house down there? Weird! You never know what you'll find! And snow? I don't know. It's just always like this." Tu explained. "But who are you? And how did you get under my world?"

"Under your world? There's snow up there?!" The words leaped out of Sammy's mouth as if the sounds themselves were reaching to see what was up there.

"Sure! Come on up! But first, will you please hand Ralph to me? I promise he won't scratch or bite. Will ya, Ralph?"

"Meorf!" said Ralph with a big puppy-cat smile.

Sammy took Ralph gently in his hands, climbed back onto the dresser, and handed him up to Tu. Tu smiled and carefully lifted Ralph back into the strange world above. Finally, Tu reached down for Sammy, and Sammy reached up for Tu. Their hands clasped around each other's wrists, and Sammy was pulled up, up, up.

5.

"What is this place called?!" Sammy gasped in wistful wonder.

It wasn't even dinner time, but he found himself under a night sky that was filled with twinkling swirls of stars. Blue and orange planets hung in the sky, some with glowing rings around them. It was a quiet so pure. Sammy and Tu stood in a wide, snowy field. Hills of snow-covered evergreen trees stretched out, out, and on.

"This place would never burn down," Sammy mumbled. Then in a full voice he asked again, "Tu, what is this place called?"

"Hm," said Tu, like he had never thought about it before. "I don't know. What would you call it?"

"Well, I would call it the attic, but attics don't usually have their own sky. Usually there's a roof right above your head, and instead of a snowy forest there's just some old boxes and fuzzy stuff on the wall."

"I like it," said Tu. "Welcome to...The Attic," he announced, dramatically sweeping his hand in front of him, as if to point across all the land and sky.

Sammy was utterly confused but too excited to worry. He was so full of questions!

"Tu! How long have you lived here? Where is your family? And are you named after the number 2?"

"Hm," said Tu again, as if he had never considered any of these things until this moment. "It's funny. I don't really remember anything before I met you just now. Weird! Maybe my name is Spanish? No, Irish? I don't know. Hey, you still didn't tell me your name."

"Oh! I'm sorry. My name is Sammy. My family just moved here, or, down there." He pointed at the snow-covered ground. "Our whole town burned down in the forest fires this summer. It's a long story. We moved here because of my dad's brother. He works at a carpet business, and he got my dad a job putting carpet on people's floors."

"Cool! Man, I'm so glad you're here! I need a friend," said Tu. "It's lonely here, just Ralph and me. I love him, but he only knows one word. He says it in different ways, but I can only understand a bit of what he means. It would be great to have a friend I can actually talk with!"

"Yeah! I just started at a new school, and I don't know anyone here. I'd love to hang out!" Sammy sputtered.

The boys shook hands and looked into each other's wide, happy eyes.

"Heyyo, Sammy!" Dad called from below. "Dinner time! We got bean burgers and fries to celebrate your first day of school!"

Sammy looked at Tu and said, "I've got to go, but I'll come back tomorrow!"

"Awesome!" said Tu.

"Bye, Ralph!" Sammy said as he lowered himself down from The Attic.

"Meorf!" said Ralph.

Tu called out from above, "I think you and I have more in common than we know."

6.

When Sammy got the dinner table, Mom and Dad were already sitting down and talking in hushed voices.

"Hey kiddo!" Mom said in a suddenly up-beat voice. "How did your pant cuffs get wet? You look like you've been walking around in a foot of snow!"

"Hm! Weird!" said Sammy, who quickly changed the subject. "I actually did make a friend today! His name is Tu, and he's kind of starting a new life like me, and I'm his first friend here too!"

"Awesome!" said Dad. "Where did he move from?"

"He doesn't remember," Sammy said, pushing a few fries into his mouth.

"He doesn't remember where he's from, hmmmmm?" said Dad, looking down at his plate quizzically.

Sammy suddenly realized how strange the whole thing had been. A world in the attic? A kid living up there? A kid who doesn't remember anything before today? Was it a dream? No. And the cuffs on his pants were wet to prove it.

Still, it was too weird to tell Mom and Dad. They were already worried about him, saying he had been acting strangely since the fire. They would think he had lost his mind!

"Oh! Ha ha…" Sammy chuckled and tilted his head. "I mean, *I* don't remember. Ha ha ha…"

"Well I'm glad to see you smiling and hear that you found a friend already," said Mom, looking concerned. "I heard you were a little grumpy earlier. You've got me worried with these angry outbursts lately."

"Yeah," Sammy said and then got quiet for a moment. "Sometimes it's like there's a fire in my mind, and I lose track of time. It feels like it only lasts a second, but when I snap out of it, I've already done something mean. It's like an accident. I just… I feel different since we lost everything."

"I know, Honey, I know. You're actually doing a great job of dealing with what happened," said Mom. "It was hard on all of us, but I imagine it must have been hardest on you. We didn't lose *every*thing though. We still have each other, and I'm so thankful for that."

Mom smiled at Sammy and rubbed his shoulder. Sammy took a big bite of his burger and felt like maybe everything was going to be alright.

7.

Walking to the second day of school, Sammy's smile shined, and his feet bounced with each step. *Boing, boing, boing!* He had made a new friend and discovered a whole, weird world! He started to remember that school wasn't so great in Greenhill anyway. At least he had a chance to start over now. Maybe he should forget about the past like Tu did.

Ms. Crimini was standing outside the classroom door. "Good morning, Danny" she said, looking slightly more comfortable than the day before.

"Good morning, Ms. Crimini!" Sammy replied. Sammy, Stanny, Danny...it didn't matter. School didn't really matter at all. He had a whole new world--The Attic. That was the only place he could think about now.

The morning went by quickly. Sammy flipped through the stinky books and filled out his papers. He was so excited to get back to his new friend.

At recess, Sammy paced around at the edge of the playground, daydreaming about The Attic.

"Ha ha! Loser!" a voice burst in front of him. A big kid with a soccer ball crashed into one of Sammy's classmates and knocked him down.

"Why don't you watch where you're goin'? Haw haw, haw haw haw!" the big kid snarked.

Sammy reached down for the kid, and the kid reached up for Sammy. Their hands clasped around each other's wrists, and Sammy pulled him up, up, up onto his feet.

"Thanks," said the kid, embarrassed.

"You're welcome! What's your name? I'm Sammy."

"So that's your name? Ms. Crimini calls you something different every time. You're the new kid."

"Yeah. I'm the new kid," said Sammy.

"My name is Owen. I've been going to school here since kindergarten. I'll help you figure things out."

"Thanks!" said Sammy. "That would be great! First, who's the big kid that knocked you over?

"That's Sharky. His real name is Daniel Binglesworth, but everyone calls him Sharky. I only know his real name because he's been going to school here forever too. He's in the next grade up. I feel bad for him sometimes, because he's always had trouble at home. But then he knocks someone down or calls names, and I don't feel bad for him anymore. I just try to stay away," Owen explained.

"Good to know," said Sammy.

TWEEEEEEEET screeched the whistle.

"Come on. You can sit with me at lunch," said Owen.

8.

The lunchroom was chaos, just like school in Greenhill. Kids ran past Sammy in all directions as Owen led him to a table in the back corner, where some other classmates were already sitting.

"Hey everyone. This is Sammy," said Owen, introducing Sammy to the crew.

"So that's your name..." said one kid while the rest let out a long, "Ohhhhhh..."

"Yeah," said Sammy. "I'm sure glad to join your table."

Owen pointed and introduced the other kids. "This here's Elijah, and Esmeralda, Mahamadou, Anh, and James."

The kids all seemed friendly. Sammy had a feeling he had found a place to belong. He hadn't felt that way in a long time.

"So how do you like it here?" asked Anh.

"It's OK," said Sammy. "It just feels like school, I guess. My family just moved into our new house a couple weeks ago. The best part is the attic."

"Oh yeah?" said Esmeralda, scrunching her nose to adjust her glasses. "I heard sometimes people find a dead body in the attic. Is there a dead body up there?"

"Or pirate treasure?!" burst Elijah.

"Or a doorway to another dimension?" asked Mahamadou.

Sammy laughed a little. "Well actually…"

"Who's this *loser*?" said a thundercloud voice from above.

They turned and saw Sharky looming overhead. He stared down at Sammy.

"I said, what's your name, loser? Or is it just 'Loser'? Ah haw haw haw hawww!" Sharky snarled.

"M…my name is…" Sammy stuttered.

"Loser. Your name is 'Loser'. Welcome to our school, Loser." Sharky got down even closer to Sammy's face. "I'm gonna make you feel right...at...home...Loser."

Sharky bellowed, "Ah haw haw haw haw hawww!" and walked away.

After Sharky left, everyone's body relaxed and the kids all let out a deep, long breath. Except for Sammy, who was still trembling with fear and anger.

"What a jerk!" Sammy said. "How does he get away this?"

Mahamadou sighed, "I think the teachers have all given up. They've been trying to help him since he was a little kid."

"Clean up your tables!" shouted Mr. Derby, the lunchroom worker. "Come on! Let's go! Jimmy! Let's go! I've asked you three times already!"

Sammy went back to class and sat at his desk, boiling with anger, hurt, and too many thoughts.

"Andy," said Ms. Crimini. "Andy?"

Sammy noticed she was looking at him.

"Sammy, Ms. Crimini. My name is Sammy," he said with a sizzling edge to his voice, trying not to let it burst into flames.

Some kids giggled.

"Oh yes, I'm sorry Sandy. Sandy, which strategy did you use to solve the division problem?"

9.

"And after he got in my face and called me 'Loser' ten times, the teacher called me a wrong name again! Twice!"

It felt good to be back in The Attic, Tu sitting at his side, stars shooting through the deep, deep sky. Sammy was still upset, but he felt much better having a friend he could talk to about it.

"Man! Rough day!" said Tu. "I'm sorry bro. That's so cool that you made a bunch of friends though! You're still the only other kid I've ever seen!"

"Meorf!" said Ralph.

"Ralph, you know I love you, but you're not a kid. It's just different," said Tu.

"I got mad again." Sammy said. "I didn't lose control, but it was close. I almost raged at Ms. Crimini! That would be big trouble. Hey, Tu, do you even go to school?"

"School? Oh hmmm," Tu said thoughtfully. "Hey! I want to show you something!"

Tu started running up a big snowy hill. Ralph ran right behind, but since the snow was taller than him, it looked like Tu was being followed by puffs of snow jumping off the ground. Sammy was close behind them both.

It was a long, steep climb. Sammy enjoyed the stillness and silence of the endless night. It was a peace so deep and sweet like a cake, lightly iced with the sound of soft footsteps in snow.

Finally they reached the top of the hill and looked around. The planets hummed with such vibrant color and looked so close that Sammy reached out, thinking he could touch them. But his hand only moved through the cool night air. The planets were still far, far away.

"Look what I got!" said Tu, holding a sled in each hand.

"Awesome!" said Sammy. "But why do you have two of them if you're the only kid in The Attic?

"That's funny! I don't know! But I *do* know I'll beat you to the bottom of this hill."

Tu threw a sled on the ground in front of Sammy.

"Ready, set...

Goooo

       ooo

          oo

             o

               o

                 o

                   o

                     o

                        ooo!"

They flew down the hill, as if the snow was open sky! Rushing so fast, Sammy felt a sudden sadness, and then the greatest happiness in the world, so happy he would cry if he wasn't laughing, free. He remembered, for just a moment, all the feelings he had been holding so tightly, and then he let them all go, falling behind him, spilling out in each laugh.

10.

When Sammy finally lay in bed that night, he felt so much lighter and cooler than when he stormed out of school in the afternoon. But then Sammy remembered that tomorrow he would be trapped in school again with that rotten Sharky. That rotten…

"Hey, what's that?" he thought.

The floor seemed to be rumbling.

Sammy switched on his light and got up from his bed. As he walked to the corner where the sound came from, he noticed something odd about the floor. There was a square piece of wood, different from the long boards across the rest of the floor. It was just about the size of the door to The Attic.

Sammy slowly turned back, lay in bed, and switched the light back off.

"I must've been having some kind of nightmare," he told himself, and he fell asleep, pretending he didn't smell the slightest bit of smoke.

11.

On the third day of school, Sammy just walked to school. There was no bounce, no flop, just a steady and thoughtful walk. He had so many things to think about, ideas glowing like coals in his mind: new friends, sledding in The Attic, Sharky, the odd rumbling from his bedroom floor. Sammy wanted to make sense of it all.

"Good morning, Randy," said Ms. Crimini.

Sammy ignored her, took his seat, and opened his stinky book.

When lunch came Sammy was glad to sit with his new friends.

"So where are you from, Sammy," Anh asked.

"I'm from a town called Greenhill. Well, I don't think it's a town anymore. It burned in the fires this summer."

"Oh, wow!" said Owen. "I saw the forest fires on the news! And the smoke came all the way here and made our sky dirty for a week!"

"Yeah," said Sammy, while crunching down a carrot. "It all came so fast. My dad came in my room and told me I had to pack my most important things in my backpack and get in the car right away. When we drove away from our house, there was fire on both sides of the road, and there was so much smoke my mom could hardly see the road enough to drive."

"Did you see any dead bodies?" asked Esmeralda.

"No. No dead bodies. Actually, do you all mind if we talk about something else? I don't really feel like talking about it right now."

"Hey loser!" said a dark, smokey voice over the table. "Or is your name idiot? Or maybe turd? I heard the teacher doesn't even know your name though, so it must just be 'Loser'! Haw haw haw haw haw!"

All the other kids, the kids he thought were his new friends, started to giggle and snort.

"Ah haw haw haw haw…" cackled Sharky as he walked away.

"I thought you were my friends!" Sammy shouted. He stood up. "I thought you were my friends! And now you're laughing at me?! That makes you just as bad as Sharky!"

"Wait, Sammy," said Mahamadou. "We're not…"

"YES, YOU ARE!" Sammy shouted at the top of his lungs. He picked up his drink and threw it at the wall as hard as he could. He picked up his apple and threw it at the wall as hard as he could, and then his sandwich and everything else.

"You! Kid!" shouted Mr. Derby. "You get over here RIGHT NOW and clean that up!"

Sammy walked right out of the lunchroom. He was so angry, he felt like his whole body was on fire. He didn't even know where he was going in this strange new school. He walked down the unknown hallways, turning here and there, anywhere. He finally found a nook at the end of a dim hallway, a place he hoped he could be alone.

Sammy sat down on the floor and cried from somewhere deep, deep in his guts. He thought of so many things that hurt and didn't make any sense. In his mind he saw Sharky, the kids laughing, Ms. Crimini, his parents worried faces, his stuffed animals that he'd kept since he was young but had to leave behind to burn with the rest of his life. He felt like the real Sammy had burned with them, and somehow he was a stranger in his own body, in a new life that wasn't his own. He sobbed harder.

At last Sammy was all cried out, and the fire inside was gone. He stood up from the floor and started walking, not knowing where.

"You! There you are!" It was Mr. Derby. "I've been looking for you all over! You're going to come back and clean up that mess you made!"

Sammy silently followed. Mr. Derby handed him a mop.

"I'm sorry Mr. Derby," Sammy said. "I didn't know what was happening until I had already done it."

"Now you clean this up. I'm going to go tell Principal Ali I found you. Get to work!" Mr. Derby seemed more like an army sergeant than a lunchroom worker.

"Principal Ali!" thought Sammy. "What have I done? Now Mom and Dad are going to be worried *and* mad at me!"

Sammy mopped up his orange juice. His brain wanted to worry, but it was too tired. It felt wet and soggy like the mop.

12.

Sammy sat in the principal's office. Principal Ali's face was the opposite of Ms. Crimini's. Her mouth was drawn tight and serious, but her eyes smiled.

"It's nice to finally meet you, Sammy." Principal Ali said. "It's too bad it had to be like this."

Sammy's mom sat next to him. No part of her face was smiling. She was quiet, upset, and thinking intensely about what to do.

"I understand you had a very hard time this summer, Sammy," said Principal Ali. "I imagine it must have been very scary and painful, and moving to a new school can be very difficult, even under the best circumstances."

They sat in silence for a few moments. Sammy looked out the window, which opened onto the front of the school yard. He saw Sharky standing at the curb, waiting to get picked up.

"Oh, that rotten jerk!" he thought. "He started this! Why isn't he in here instead of me!"

Principal Ali broke the silence and spoke again.

"Of course, you can't shout and throw things in the cafeteria. Mr. Derby says you did a nice job of cleaning it up though. I think you've made restoration."

"What's restoration?" Sammy asked.

"Restoration. That's when you restore things, when you fix the damage that you caused. I don't want to punish students. I just want to heal the harm and help you learn to make a better choice the next time you get angry. Does that make sense?" she asked.

"Yes," Sammy said.

Mom was still quiet and thoughtful, but she seemed to agree

with how Principal Ali wanted to handle the situation.

"But why doesn't Sharky have to make restoration?" Sammy asked. "Why isn't he in here?"

"Sammy, I will have a meeting with Sharky, er, Daniel tomorrow morning. But unfortunately neither I nor Mr. Derby saw what happened before you started throwing things. I have asked Mr. Derby to pay closer attention if Daniel starts walking over to you. I can't tell you details, but let's just say that he has been through some challenges too. And I will also hold him accountable for his actions as much as I can, so he can do restoration and make better choices."

"That jerk," thought Sammy, looking out the window at Sharky again. "He got away with it!"

Sammy saw some big kids, even bigger than Sharky, walk across the school yard. They said something to Sharky. Sharky put his head down and looked away. One of the big kids got right up close to Sharky. He spit right on Sharky's face. All the big kids started laughing and walked away.

Sammy couldn't believe his eyes! The bully he was so scared of, who he felt such burning anger against, just got spit on by really big kids! And Sammy got to watch it happen!

Sammy felt a rush of excitement and revenge. But it fell quickly into sadness. Sammy almost felt like someone had spit in his own face. And as Sharky wiped off the spit and hung his head low, Sammy felt a little like crying.

"So, Sammy," said his mother.

"Yeah, mom?" Sammy said.

"Next time you get mad, why don't you do your breathing like we practiced and walk away if you need to. And, Principal Ali, I trust you'll be protecting my son from bullies?" Mom's question sounded more like a demand.

"Yes. You have my word. I want Sammy to feel safe, comfortable, and happy here in his new school. We will do whatever it takes to protect him and foster his sense of belonging."

"Very good," said Mom. "Thank you, Principal Ali. Okay, Sammy. Let's go home.

13.

"It was so weird!" said Sammy.

"Sounds like it!" said Tu.

"Meorf!" said Ralph.

"I hate him! I hate his guts! But I can't help feeling bad for him. I can't help caring!" Sammy went on.

"Maybe anger and caring are two sides of one feeling. Maybe every feeling has two sides!" Tu wondered. "Maybe you two more in common than either of you knows."

"Maybe." said Sammy, thinking deeper. "The car ride home with Mom

was so weird. She didn't really talk much. I thought she was going to be furious! She just seemed quiet and worried though. I never got sent to the principal's office in Greenhill. I thought that was only for bad kids! Tu, am I a bad kid now?"

"Hm. I think there's no such thing as bad kids or good kids, just kids," said Tu.

"I guess. But what am I going to do if Sharky picks on me again? Am I really just going to do my breathing and walk away?" said Sammy.

"Why not?" said Tu.

"Because then he wins! He gets to be a bully, and I get to be upset. It's not fair!"

"But if you flip out again, and he still doesn't get in trouble, you lose again," Sammy reasoned. "I don't know dude. I don't see a way out, but I'm sure you'll find it somehow."

Sammy and Tu laid on their backs in the snow, with Ralph snuggling between them. All three gazed at the marvelous sky, each having thoughts of their own.

"Tu, sometimes I get scared of my own anger. I didn't decide to shout and throw things. One second everyone was laughing at me, and the next I was running away down the hall. I don't like losing control. Have you ever been scared of yourself?" Sammy asked.

"No," said Tu, "but it's OK if you feel that way. I'm not scared of you."

"Thanks" said Sammy with a smile.

14.

Once again Sammy felt better after an evening in The Attic. He seemed to understand things better too. Still, he had a mystery inside that he needed to solve. What was this anger that had so much power over him? How could he sometimes not be himself? What could happen if he got really, really angry and lost control for more than a few seconds? Maybe he would come to his senses and find out that he had burned the whole school down!

Sammy lay there wondering in the dark when he heard the rumble coming from below, louder than the night before.

"I am definitely not asleep," Sammy told himself. "And I definitely smell smoke!"

Sammy leaped out of bed and ran to the rumbling corner of the floor. He ran his fingers around the square floorboard, feeling a little space between its edge and the other boards. He pushed his fingers into the narrow gap and felt the square tilt slightly out of place. Sammy lifted the wooden square away. He looked down at a stone stairway leading deep into the ground. And smoke was pouring out.

Sammy ran down the stairs, toward the smoke. He was terrified, but he knew he had to do something!

The bottom of the stairs led into a forest. Thick smoke filled the air, but the flames hadn't reached this part of the forest yet. He saw the fire flashing against the trees further into the woods. Sammy ran towards the fire.

Sammy got closer to the fire and realized there was just one tree burning. Walking even closer, he discovered it wasn't a tree on fire. It was a boy. The boy wasn't burning up though. He was making the fire. He was the fire. The flames were coming out of his eyes, and they spewed out his mouth as he shouted and roared in a frenzied rage.

Sammy looked on in horror, but he was so curious he took a couple of steps closer. Now he recognized the boy. It was himself.

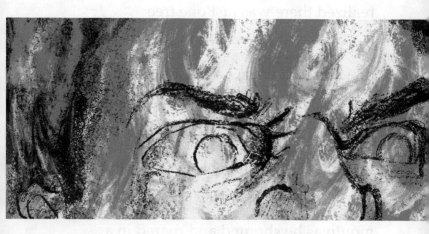

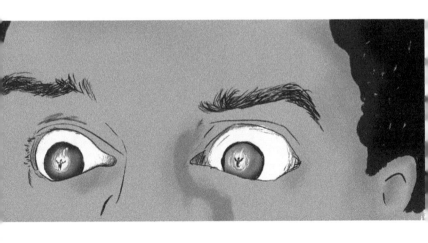

15.

Sammy sat alone at lunch. He couldn't stop thinking of his dream the night before, if it was just a dream. He could still see his other self screaming, fire swirling through him, and he could still feel his feet running away, back up the stairs. And here at school Sammy was all on his own again. It felt like his new group of friends had already burned down.

Mahamadou walked over.

"Sammy," Mahamadou started, "Man…"

"Forget about it," said Sammy .
"Just leave me alone. I don't need any
fake friends."

"Dude, we weren't laughing at
you. I promise!"

"Whatever."

"For real, we were laughing
about how Ms. Crimini can't remember
anything. And then we imagined her
calling out 'turd' in class. And we were
all so nervous with Sharky there, we
just cracked up, and it just turned into a
mess. I promise we weren't laughing at
you. We're not like that. We've all been
picked on by Sharky too. We know how
it is."

Sammy felt like Mahamadou
really meant what he said. He sat and
thought, and soon he felt like some new

green shoots were growing up through the fresh ashes of friendship.

"Alright." Sammy said. "I guess I understand." He got up and sat with his crew again.

"I'm sorry Sammy," they all said, almost at the same time.

"Yeah, I'm sorry too," said Sammy. "I just felt like everyone was against me, and I guess I lost control."

"We know," said Elijah "Hey, what was it like in the principal's office?"

"Yeah! Did she yell at you?" asked Anh.

"I heard she has dead bodies in there. Did you see any dead bodies?" asked Esmeralda, fidgeting her glasses with her nose.

"Actually it was OK. She didn't yell or bring out dead bodies. She said it was good enough that I apologized and cleaned the mess I made, and that I need to make a better choice next time I'm mad. But it's so hard when he's such a jerk! Owen, you said Sharky had trouble at home. What kind of trouble?"

"Well, I only know what other kids have said, and some things I overheard from my parents. But ever since we were little, his parents fought a lot, and it sounds like his dad would get mad and leave a lot."

"Yeah," said Esmeralda. "And last year his parents got divorced. And I think he sees his dad even less now."

"Well, well, well," a voice rumbled over the table. "Hey loser! Did you have fun in the principal's office? Haw haw haw haw! And you snitched on me, you little loser! I'll teach you not to do that again."

Sammy clenched his fists and started to do his breathing. "In. One… two… three…. Out. One… two… three. In…"

"And you're sitting with the kids who were laughing at you just yesterday? You're an even bigger loser than I thought! Haw haw haw haw haw haw!" Sharky taunted.

Sammy stood up to walk away, but Sharky blocked his path and got in his face. Sammy couldn't take it anymore. He thought of the worst, most hurtful thing he could possibly say. And he said it.

"Yeah? Well at least my dad wants me, you big jerk!" Sammy shouted.

Mr. Derby started walking over, but it was too late.

"Oh yeah?" Sharky shouted with eyes of pain and rage. "My dad said he's picking me up *today* after school, and we're gonna go to the football game together, you loser!" Then, he spat right on Sammy's face.

Sammy didn't know how he got there, but he was on top of Sharky, punching him in the face again and again and again.

16.

"Sammy, Sammy, Sammy," said Principal Ali. And then she said nothing for a long time.

Sammy's Mom sat next to him again, also saying nothing for a long time.

Sammy looked out the window, and there was Sharky again. He thought to himself, "Look! He got away with it again! And now he gets to go to the football game with his dad!"

"Principal Ali," Sammy whimpered, "Why isn't Sharky in here

again? He spit on me and everyone saw it!"

"Yes, Sammy. And I will be calling his family as soon as our meeting is over, and I will meet with them tomorrow. I'll tell you more about that in a minute. We need to talk about what you did first."

"Sammy," Principal Ali continued, "Please consider the difference. He spit on you, which is disgusting and hurtful, and that should have never happened to you. But you tackled him and hit him in the face so many times that Mr. Derby lost count." She paused. "That kind of violence, and the way you lost all self-control...well, we need to discuss it right away." Her mouth became a harder frown than usual, but her eyes softened into an even deeper smile.

Sammy's mom shook her head, as if she agreed with Principal Ali, but wished she didn't.

"And I've also invited Mr. Metzger, our school counselor to this meeting so you, your mother, and he can start getting to know each other." Principal Ali went on.

There was a knock at the office door, and it opened a crack.

"May I come in?" said a warm, crisp voice.

"Please do, Mr. Metzger" said Principal Ali.

A short man with salt-and-pepper hair and beard walked in with strong, gentle steps.

"Pleased to meet you. I'm Tim," Mr. Metzger said, shaking Mom's hand and then Sammy's.

"So, Mr. Metzger you're just in time. I was just going to tell Sammy and his mother about tomorrow." Principal Ali said. "Tomorrow, Sammy, you are suspended from school."

Sammy's jaw dropped, but no sound could come out.

Mom pursed her lips. She stopped shaking her head and started to nod a little bit.

"But," Principal Ali continued, "I would like you to come back tomorrow afternoon with your mother, your father, or both of them if possible. I would like us to have a restorative meeting with Daniel and his mother."

"Yes," Mr. Metzger continued. "We want to face the problem directly, in a loving way, a way that helps you and Daniel learn how to deal with pain and anger."

"Did he just say 'loving'?!" thought Sammy. He couldn't believe his ears! Sammy turned and looked out the window again. Sharky was still standing outside, waiting to get picked up, but it was getting dark, and droplets of September rain began to fall.

"So what does this meeting look like?" asked Mom.

"Well, it's pretty simple really." said Mr. Metzger. "First we talk about what happened. We don't try to explain why it happened. We don't assign

blame. We just want to agree on the basic facts. It's amazing what happens! Simply by discussing the basic facts, I think both boys will start to understand it all more deeply."

"Next, we talk about the feelings each of them had, and both of the boys will understand how they were both harmed. Usually they see that they have more in common than they thought. Finally, we discuss what would need to happen for true restoration. The boys will come up with their own ideas about that, and hopefully they'll agree to something by the end of the meeting. In my experience, they almost always do."

Sammy looked out the window again. A car finally pulled up and

Sharky got in. But it wasn't his dad. It was his mom. Sharky's head bowed over and it looked like...was he crying? Was Sharky crying?!

The big, horrible monster was crying! Sammy began to imagine if his own dad stopped coming home. Maybe Sharky's life had burned down too. Sammy felt his heart ache, and his stomach was sick, and his eyes swelled with tears. Sammy worked to keep his face looking calm, but a few tears began to overflow his eyelids and slide down his cheeks.

Suddenly, Sammy burst out crying. He cried for Sharky. For a moment, it seemed that he *was* Sharky, crying there in the principal's office. He began to cry for his own life that burned down. He cried for every sad thing that ever happened to anybody, as though he held the whole world inside himself.

The grown-ups stopped talking and exchanged looks with each other quietly.

"Sammy," said Mom. "Is there anything you want to tell us."

"I'm sorry!" Sammy squeezed the words out of his mouth. "I'm just confused and scared and I don't want to hurt anybody, but I didn't know what else to do! And I still don't know what to doooo…" he sobbed.

Sammy's mom put her arms around him, giving him a big hug.

For some strange reason, Mr. Metzger smiled, looking pleased with

Sammy crying. "I believe it's already working," he smiled.

17.

"And then, just before we left, my mom stared at Principal Ali like she had lasers coming from her eyes, and she said, 'I hope this meeting works. if you can't protect my child at school, *I will*. And you might not like how I do it.'" Sammy said.

"Wow! That's crazy!" said Tu. "Man! Your mom is fierce! But, so, you started crying in front of everyone?"

"Yeah, it's embarrassing." Sammy said.

"I know it is," said Tu, "But it shouldn't be. Everyone does it!"

"It's funny," Sammy added, "Crying seems weak, and making some agreement with Sharky tomorrow seems weak too. But, I wasn't scared of Sharky when I was hitting him. I'm more nervous about just sitting in a room with him tomorrow and talking!"

Sammy and Tu climbed the big hill and rode their sleds down again and again. Sammy felt free. By the time they were laying on their backs looking at the stars again, with Ralph snuggled in between, he didn't feel nervous anymore at all.

"Tu," said Sammy, "I haven't really talked about it much, because it's hard, but, well… I can't explain how bad it hurts to have your house burn down, and all your favorite things too, and every place you know is gone, and you have to move away from all your friends, and then you're a stranger in a new life that doesn't feel like yours. I mean, it's really simple in a way, but somehow it still doesn't make any sense. Am I making any sense right now?"

"Perfect sense," said Tu. "Perfect sense."

"Thanks," said Sammy. "I guess I just needed to hear that."

Stars twinkled, swirled, and shot across the calm darkness above.

"One more thing," said Tu. "I know it's hard to stop thinking about how it's all gone, but if you can remember it's gone, can you also remember the good times too? You know, like, can you just focus on how good it was?"

"Maybe," said Sammy. "Maybe."

Sammy and Tu said goodbye, and Sammy went to bed. They would have taken longer to say goodbye if they had known it would be the last time they would ever see each other.

18.

Sammy woke up. It was still nighttime. The floor was rumbling and shaking, and smoke was coming up into his room. He switched on the light and stood up, wide awake.

Sammy pulled up the floorboard and ran down the stairs into the forest.

He ran and ran, getting closer to the fire. He knew what he had to do.

Sammy got to the clearing where his other self stood blazing in the smoky night.

"Get away from me!" his other self shouted. "Stay back! I'll burn you if you get any closer! I'll burn you just like I burn everything else!"

Sammy looked at himself. The shadows and firelight flickered across his face. He stepped forward. He stepped forward again. And again.

Sammy looked into his own angry eyes. But the anger was just a show. Behind the anger he could see scared, sad, confused Sammy. And he felt a caring sadness for himself.

Sammy stepped right into the fire and wrapped his arms around himself. Together they began to cry.

"I'm sorry I burned everything down!"

"You didn't burn anything down! It's not your fault! You can't blame yourself for this!"

"I know! But it feels like my fault!"

"It feels like your fault but it's not!"

"But why is everything gone!?"

"Forests burn sometimes! Sometimes we can't control life!"

"But everything is gone! What if we lose Mom and Dad too?! What if we die!?"

"You didn't lose Mom and Dad. And you didn't lose me! I'm right here!"

They stopped talking and just hugged each other harder, and they hugged and cried until they felt calm. The fire slowly went out, and the smoke faded from the sky.

Sammy took his arms down and stepped back. The burning Sammy was just Sammy now. They looked around, and Greenhill was just like they remembered it all their life. White clouds slowly sailed across blue sky. The rolling hills were covered in green trees, and fresh pine tingled in their noses. They saw their house. It wasn't burned. It was exactly as it was when Sammy lived there for all those years.

"Listen."

"Yeah?"

"This will always be right here, OK?

"OK."

"It's just one thought away, and it'll always be here."

"This can't burn?"

"No. Nothing can ever burn this. It's safe here. Forever"

19.

Sammy rushed home from school. He couldn't wait to tell Tu about the strangest day he ever had! He and Sharky had actually talked, almost like friends!

At first they sat there, neither one of them talking or looking at the other. But after Mr. Metzger spoke with them for a little while, Sammy could tell that he and Sharky both wanted to solve the problem. But neither one of them wanted to start, so Sammy just went ahead and started. It wasn't even complicated. He just told the truth about how painful it was, his home burning down and moving to a new school. He told Sharky how he tried to get away from him, but he didn't know what else to do when Sharky wouldn't let him go.

Sharky talked about how scary it was to have his dad get mad all the time, and then how much it hurt when his dad left, and how it feels when his dad makes so many promises and never keeps them. Sharky talked about how he feels like nobody likes him or wants to be his friend. And he picks on people to feel better. He said he doesn't know why it feels good to pick on people, but it just does, at least for a little while.

Sharky said he would stop picking on Sammy and everyone else, but he said he needed help because he doesn't know how to make friends. Sammy told him he wasn't sure exactly how to make friends either, but he could sit with the crew at lunch as long as he keeps his promise not to hurt anyone. Wow!

Sammy got home and went right to his bedroom. He had so many words pushing to get out of his mouth and into Tu's mind. He climbed up onto the dresser, opened the door to The Attic, and climbed up.

But there was no sky, no snow, no Ralph, and no Tu. It was just an old attic with some fuzzy stuff on the walls, a roof, and two old sleds.

Sammy climbed down from the attic and closed the door. He got in bed and cried himself to sleep.

Epilogue

It was late January, and Sam was driving through his old hometown. Well, one of his hometowns. His family moved there after the fires that took Greenhill. He was passing by on the highway that night and decided to stop and have a quick look around.

Sam pulled into his old neighborhood. A lot had changed. Some houses were gone. There were many more new ones. His old house was still standing, barely.

The house was partly burned down. The main structure stood, but one wall of the house was mostly gone, and the siding was blackened from soot. Sam got out of the car. His feet crunched the snow and memories poured through his mind. He remembered how sad and confused he had been when his family first moved in. He felt sad for his little Sammy.

Sam stepped over a snow drift and walked in the front door, which was only hanging by one hinge. He walked to his old bedroom. He climbed up on an old, charred desk, and opened the door to the attic. He climbed up.

Sam found himself under a night sky that was filled with twinkling swirls of stars. It was a quiet so pure, and hills of snow-covered evergreen trees stretched out, out, and on.

The fire had burned off most of the roof. Sam looked around at the snow-covered attic, with two, snow-covered sleds, and then looked back up at the open sky. Sam thought he heard a little "meorf!" from the corner. He didn't look, but he smiled.

Sam had gained much over the years, and he had lost much too. Now he knew that forest fires are part of nature's normal cycle. He had learned that many forest fires these days were caused by pollution, but some forest fires had always happened. He had learned that nature needs forest fires to make space for new life to grow.

It was right here in this old attic that Sam had first learned how to deal with the pain of losing a life and the pain of getting a new one. It was right here that he learned every old life lives on inside him, unchanged in his memory. He had been many different Sams in his life already. And he was grateful for all of them.

About the Author

Ben Gallup is a writ...wait...that's just weird.

I am a writer, visual artist, musician, and school librarian (among other things). *Sammy's Attic* is my first book aimed to kids. *Sammy's Attic* was written in Seattle, Washington and completed in Stuttgart, Germany, where I currently live. I'm you in a different human suit. If you want to find me, you will.